Ione

KINK, Volume 6

S L Davies

Published by S L Davies, 2023.

IONE

First edition. January 2, 2023.

Copyright © 2023 S L Davies.

ISBN: 979-8215825501

Written by S L Davies.

sucking on a pacifier. It was comforting. But that didn't make me sick. The feeling of having someone caring for me and the surface of the diaper around my cock felt good. It was no different from someone who liked leather or latex. I just preferred a diaper and baby powder.

I stood from the kitchen table and went into my bedroom. I wondered what would happen if I disobeyed my father. If I just sat in my room and did nothing. I wondered what he would do. As I looked around my room, my bedroom door opened, and Mama stepped in.

She handed me an envelope. "Here, this will give you enough to get a place somewhere," she said before turning and leaving again.

I opened the envelope to see a large wad of cash. That was my answer. They were serious. Slowly I started to load my clothes and anything I didn't want to leave behind, like my stuffies, into a duffle bag before going out to my car. Looking back at the house, I saw Mama standing in the window. I lifted my hand in a wave, but she turned her around. My heart cracked open, and I sighed before climbing into my car and bringing the engine to life.

I pulled out of the driveway as tears started to fall and drip from my chin. Where was I going to go? I remembered a post I'd seen on the Facebook group that I belonged to about a club in Lalbert where they had a large littles room. I reached out for my phone and opened my maps. I input Lalbert into the GPS and saw that I was only three hours away.

Pointing the car in that direction, I followed the map as tears flowed steadily down my cheeks. I needed to be with people like me. People that understood. People that knew there was nothing wrong with me. I wasn't sick.

Chapter One

one

Club KINK was by far the best club I'd ever attended. Asher catered to everyone, and I'd never felt so safe. I'd tried Hellfire, but that place was full of sleazebags, and I could never fully immerse myself in my little side. There was just one thing I was missing. A Daddy or a Mommy. I wanted someone to call my own. It was fun to play, and I had a lot of friends at the club; sometimes, we caught up on the outside and played together. But I wanted someone special. I liked that person I could come home to after a full day at work and relax, knowing Daddy or Mommy had all my needs taken care of.

At the club, I saw littles ranging in age; some were babies, wore diapers, sucked on a pacifier, and even wore mittens; they often climbed into the cribs and slept. Others were crawling stage and liked to keep the Daddies and Mommies who came into the room on their toes.

Then there were the toddlers. I was a toddler. I liked to color, paint and run around with my friends, being loud, but then I wanted to curl up in the bean bag and listen to a story while someone played with my hair and helped me to wind down. Jade, my best friend since college, was a little too.

I was absolutely floored the day she admitted it all to me. As it happened, we were in the same dorm, and I'd forgotten to put my pacifier away after I'd used it the night before. Jade came bounding into my room as she often did, and her eyes seemed to zero in on the bright pink paci. My cheeks had flamed with embarrassment, almost as red as my hair. I tried to think of an excuse as to why it was there, but Jade knew I didn't have brothers or sisters. She knew that I didn't have any kids around. So, I stood there stammering until she looked at me with wide eyes.

"You're a little?" she asked.

I bit into my bottom lip and nodded my head. A huge smile spread across her face as she bounced excitedly. "Me too," she screamed before pulling me into a tight hug. From then on, we'd been even closer, more like sisters than best friends. We explored different clubs and met others in the community. But it wasn't until we'd finished university and started working that we met Einar and Brandt. Einar was able to pick us up straight away. He came to me one day while I was typing away and quietly put a flyer on my desk. When I lifted it, I saw it was for Club KINK, and they were holding a littles night.

I'd spun at my desk in shock to look at the big Yeti, but he just smiled and gave me a wink. Jade and I had attended the littles night and never looked back. We had more than being littles in common; Jade and I were both witches. As it turned out, our mamas had grown up in the same coven but had been killed during a fire at the home in which they lived. I didn't know the whole story, as the coven was wiped out. Mama and Jade's Mama had just managed to get us out before the fire ripped through the place. Taking with it all of the other coven members.

We were found by two members of the Lalbert Fire, and while I was put into the foster system, Jade had been adopted. I didn't understand why I never got adopted, but it was what it was. I didn't have a bad life. I wasn't abused or anything like many others was. I just didn't have a forever family like Jade had. When I turned eighteen, I went to Lalbert University, studied marketing, and got a job in Winchester at Flourish Advertising. It wasn't anything special. I was still young and working my way up the ladder. But I enjoyed what I did.

I never knew my Papa. I don't know if he was also killed in the fire. I'd always assumed he was. Jade had researched our family histories when we discovered the connection, but both of our fathers were a mystery. As it turned out, our coven's records were also destroyed in the fire. I was sure there would be a way to find out, but I didn't really care enough. I was busy living my life. It was how I lived every day. I focused on the now rather than the past.

But I found myself more and more focusing on the future. Jade wasn't interested in finding a Daddy; she was happy to just go to the club and play. We had a lot of little friends. But I was different from Jade. It wasn't enough for me. I wanted a Daddy or a Mommy.

"So, Ranris, Gren, Sor, Gretel, Deron, Tabby, and Triban have all RSVP'd," Jade said with a giggle. She'd been planning her twenty-fifth birthday party since last year. Asher would let her hold the party in the littles room at the club. He said that he would organize streamers and a birthday cake too. I think March, his mate, would be helping him manage the room, but I couldn't wait.

"What about Millie and Frenita?" I asked.

"Oh yes, I got Millie's RSVP yesterday through email; I almost forgot. Thank you for reminding me. And I spoke to Elm and Acat; they are bringing Yucca and Essia as well, not that they will be able to join in with the games as they are just babies."

I shrugged my shoulders. "They might like to listen to the music and watch us play. Have you thought about games?"

Jade's smile was contagious. "Asher said that he'd talked with Nash and will organize the games."

"Is Maddox coming too?"

Jade sighed and shook her head. "No. He has to work, he has been swamped lately, and I'm worried about him. I think Nash is too."

I sighed. I knew how busy the panda shifter was. But I also knew that Nash took good care of him. Nash was active, too; there was going to be a war against the Nephilim, Ettore. Nash had been busy with that at work. But I was glad to hear he would take some time off to attend Jade's birthday party.

"What other Mommies and Daddies are coming?" I asked.

Jade shrugged her shoulders. "I don't know. Asher said that Tanya might come, and he said that a Daddy joined the other week. His name is Lennon. He is a phoenix shifter."

"Oh, that's cool. I wonder if he would shift for us so we could play with him?"

Jade snorted and shrugged again. "I don't know. Don't phoenixes shoot fire?"

I threw my head back and laughed hard, rolling onto my back on the soft carpet of the living room where we were sitting. I was getting excited about Jade's party. We'd been so busy at work I needed to the downtime.

Chapter Two

L ennon

"Welcome to Club KINK," Asher, the owner said as he brought me back into the main room. "It's great to have another Daddy here. Actually, I could use your help if you'd be willing?"

"Of course," I replied. I moved to Lalbert for work two weeks ago. I'd got a job with Olympian Fitness as a personal trainer and had mentioned to Beau that I was looking for somewhere to make friends and meet new people. I didn't know how Beau did it, but he'd asked me what my kinks were. When I told him I was a Daddy, he introduced me to Club KINK, and I joined.

"Great. One of the littles, Jade, is having a birthday party Saturday night in the littles room. One of the other Daddies, Nash, would be running the games for the littles attending, but he's a cop with the AJE Authority and busy now."

I nodded my head. I knew how busy the AJE Authority was. My brother was a cop in Sydney with the AJE Authority. Being phoenix shifters, we were sought after in those roles. I'd thought briefly about becoming a cop when I was younger. But it didn't suit me. I always felt like my heart was too soft. I wasn't the stereotypical alpha. I was gentle and had so much love and nurturing to give. That was why I chose to become a personal trainer instead. I could help people who wanted to lose weight or gain strength. I could provide them with that nurture that they decided.

"Yeah, that sounds like a lot of fun. How many littles are there?" I asked.

Asher hummed. "I think if you prepare for around fifteen, then you will be safe. I know that Jade has invited some, but I suspect we will have others come that might not be regulars or in case we get some new littles."

"How many Mommies and Daddies are regulars now?"

Asher runs his hand down over his beard. "There are six, seven including yourself. However, they aren't all regulars. Acat and Elm come with their littles every Saturday night. Tanya comes regularly, but Nash can't often come due to work. His little mate is Maddox."

"Oh yeah, now I know what you're talking about; I know Maddox."

Asher smiled and nodded his head. "He's a lovely guy but likes to keep his little side private."

"I get that. I don't often talk about my kinks, either. I'd made that mistake in college and got chased out for being a pedo."

Asher growled in his throat and curled his lip. "Narrow-minded people are the worst. The other Mommies and Daddies are Bodhi, Michael, and Erin. Bodhi tries to get here every fortnight, and Erin comes around about once a month. They both are pretty busy. Bodhi is a nurse, which keeps him flat out, and I'm not sure what Erin does; it's something to do with the government, so she plays when she can. Michael is a social worker, and his little is Tabby, from Tabbies café."

I knew the place. "Best burgers in the world. I didn't realize that she was a little."

Asher chuckled. "Watch her long enough, and it will become pretty obvious."

I grinned and nodded my head. I was going to have to take better notice next time.

"Alright, I'll come up with some party games to play."

Asher grinned and patted me on the back. "Excellent. The littles are going to have a great time. I've promised to supply party food and March, my mate, is going to help me decorate the room with streamers and balloons.

"How old is Jade when she is in little space?"

"Three."

"Does she have specific colors she favors?" I nodded my head. That was a great age, I would make sure I bought her a gift.

Asher chuckled. "Yep. Orange. She is obsessed with the color."

The other day, I saw a stuffie in the toy shop a bright orange lion. I grinned. "Perfect. I'll have to grab it to give her as a present."

"She'd love that. I hope you're ready. The toddler littles are wild, and they will be bouncing off the walls when they have a belly full of sugar."

I snorted. "I'll be okay."

"Have you had a little of your own?"

I sighed and nodded my head as I thought about Benjamin. "Yeah. We broke up about three years ago."

Asher winced. "I take it from that tone it wasn't a mutual breakup?"

I shook my head. "No. I discovered Benjamin cheating on me with a guy from our old club in Sydney. It was why I moved here. I couldn't stay in Sydney anymore. Everything was a reminder of Benjamin and how much he'd hurt me. So, I sold everything I couldn't fit in my car and moved here."

"I'm sorry that you went through that. Do you think you'd like to meet little of your own?"

I nodded. "Yeah, I am open to it. I did a lot of work and have released the anger I felt towards Benji. I'm finally ready to move on and find someone new."

Asher smiled. "Well, I hope you find that little for yourself."

I smiled in return. "Thanks, man. I best be off, I've got work soon, but I'll see you Saturday night if you are around."

Asher grinned. "Yeah, we have a babysitter for this weekend, so March and I are coming to play."

"Great. See you then."

As I walked out of the club, I felt like I had a new pep. I think I'd found my new home. I couldn't wait for Saturday and meeting the littles that belonged to the club.

Chapter Three

Tanya

"Are you working Saturday night?" Aina asked as I walked back into the staff cafeteria after having to ditch our lunch to take an emergency phone call that wasn't an emergency at all.

I yawned and shook my head. "Nope. I am taking the night off to go to the club."

Aina grinned. "Awesome, it's about time you let your hair down and relaxed for a bit."

I sighed. I'd been working flat chat for months now. I got to the club as often as possible, but my sex life and kinks had to sit by the wayside. It felt like we were having more and more casualties needing emergency surgery coming in, and I didn't understand why. They were a mix of humans and supernatural, but it felt like we were busier than usual.

"It's been a rough few months," I replied as I took a large gulp of my now lukewarm coffee.

Aina nodded her head. "Yeah, I spend more time here than at home."

"How is everything going home?"

Aina's smile was dreamy as she thought about her mates. She was so in love with them, and I couldn't be happier for her. They treated her like the queen she was.

"It's been amazing. Decker is flourishing, as is Dan. I can't believe how lucky I got. How is Neveah doing?"

My sister was quadriplegic after a car accident she was involved in with Mama and Papa. Neveah had been the only survivor. With the number of hours I worked, I needed specialized care for her, so I had her in a school, but I quickly learned that not all schools are good beneath the shiny surface. Neveah was being left in her filth; she had the worst nappy rash I'd ever seen. Not to mention that she was seventeen years old and humiliated that she was covered in her waste.

"She is doing a lot better. I couldn't be happier living out on the Devil's Advocates compound. Amos has been fantastic with her," I replied. Amos, the mate of one of the Devil's Advocates, Jasper, was a special needs teacher and had taken Neveah under his wing.

After the attack on the place last month, I'd considered moving away. I didn't want to put Neveah in any kind of danger. Thankfully, she'd been in class with Amos when the fire came through, and he was able to get her to safety. Now that the gods were living amongst us on the compound, I felt safer.

"She is getting along with the other kids?" Aina asked.

"Yeah, it took her a little while to get used to it. And the other kids at first weren't sure how to cope with her, but she has found her little group. She and Autumn are as thick as thieves."

Aina smiled. "That's fantastic. I'm so happy for her and you. All you need now is a little of your own, and your life will be complete."

I sighed and leaned back in my chair, drinking the last coffee. "Wouldn't that just be the icing on the cake?"

Aina chuckled. "No one at the club taking your eye?"

I shrugged my shoulders. "I have a couple that I play with while I'm at the club, but I don't know if they are anything more than that."

"Well, I guess you'll never know who will join."

"That's true. Are you going to be there on Saturday?"

Aina nodded her head. "Yep. We've all got the day off; Anghus has offered to watch Decker for the night. Apparently, they are doing some more training with Artemis," Aina shook her head and laughed. "It still blows my mind to walk into a room and see a god sitting at the table like it is completely normal."

I snorted and nodded my head. "I know what you mean. I walked into the dining room, and Frigg sat at the table chatting with Odin. Odin looks up, grins at me, and says, hello. I didn't know if I was meant to curtsy, bow, or what. I just replied hi and quickly got out of there."

Aina threw her head back and laughed. "It's been such an eye-opener. I'm actually going to miss them if they go back to Middle Earth after the war."

I nodded my head. "I think Neveah will too. She has been learning a lot from Hel and Athena."

"Have you asked them whether they would heal her?"

"Apparently, Iver asked, but they said that although they could, they weren't willing to because one change here can cause a reaction elsewhere. Neveah had been a little disappointed, but she understood."

Aina sighed and nodded her head. "It's a shame."

I shrugged. "Yeah, it is, but I don't want to be the reason that someone else ends up in a wheelchair or something else."

"That's true. So, I heard it was Jade's birthday party on Saturday night."

I laughed and nodded as I thought about the little blonde-haired witch who had been so excited to tell me it was her birthday and give me my invitation that she'd made herself.

"I've bought her the cutest dress; it's a purple witch outfit."

"I can see her loving that."

I smiled and nodded my head. I'd searched high and low for something that would suit the little one for her birthday, and the minute I laid eyes on the outfit, I knew it was perfect. Purple was Jade's favorite color, and the outfit perfectly matched between witch and princess. Just like Jade.

Chapter Four

A usten

I pulled into Lalbert and sighed. First, I needed somewhere to stay, then I would have to find a job. Shit, I hadn't even had a chance to tell my boss that I would no longer work there. I scrubbed my hand down over my face, my tears had finally dried about halfway into the trip, but that niggle in my stomach hadn't left. I felt sick that my parents could possibly think I was ill. It was a question I'd gone over and over in my mind since I first discovered what a little meant being and how it fits with me.

I was fifteen when I discovered the joys of being a little. It wasn't about having a bad childhood or anything for me. My parents were fine. I was raised fine. I was happy. But as every teenager, I discovered the joys of online porn. While searching, I stumbled on age play, and I couldn't explain it; something struck me. It was like I found everything I ever wanted and more. I'd secretly bought a pacifier to test it out, which then progressed to diapers and stuffies. Eventually, I found that I was more of a baby who could crawl in little space.

I interacted with other age players online and met up with them occasionally to play. I'd managed to keep it a complete secret from my parents, I knew beneath it all they would never understand. But that part of my life had been secret until now.

I drove down the main street of the town of Lalbert and took in everything around me. I knew that club KINK was here somewhere. The place was pretty well known in the kink world. The owner, a bear shifter, ran the business with inclusive exclusivity. It was expensive to join, which stopped many people who just wanted to laugh at us or abuse us from attending. The money Mama gave me wasn't going to be enough to join, but I hoped that if I could get some work, I'd soon be able to afford the member fees.

I pulled into a car spot and glanced up at the café that I'd pulled up in front of. The front of the building was painted in a bright yellow, with daisies. Tabbies Café. My stomach rumbled, reminding me that I hadn't eaten since leaving home. I glanced at the clock on the dashboard and saw it was nearing six o'clock. I wondered how much longer they were going to be open. The lights were still on, and chairs were down in the shop. I climbed out of the car and walked towards the door.

"Hi there," a woman greeted me with a bright smile. "We are just closing for the night, but I can get you something light."

I shook my head. "No, bother. I just arrived in town. Is there a motel or something?"

The woman cocked her head to the side. "Yeah. Come and sit, and I'll grab a slice of pie each. Do you like apple pie?" I smiled and bounced my head up and down. Apple pie was my little favorite. "Oh, and I bet you like chocolate milkshakes," she giggled.

I nodded my head rapidly. "Yes. They are my favorite," I gushed, feeling my little wanting desperately to come out.

"Mine too, Daddy always makes them for me. He makes the best chocolate milkshakes."

"You said Daddy. Wait, Daddy? You have a daddy?"

The woman giggled again and nodded her head. "He will be here soon. He's the bestest Daddy in the whole world."

My little wasn't going to give me a choice; he was coming in fast and furious. "Do you think your Daddy would make me a chocolate milkshake too?"

The woman's eyes grew big, and she bounced her head up and down. "I'm gonna lock the door, and then I'll get us some pie, and we can eat and color until Daddy gets here."

I grinned. "What's your name?"

"Tabby. What's yours?"

"Austen," I replied. "How did you know that I was a little?"

Tabby giggled. "The way your eyes got big, and you got excited about pie," she explained as she went behind the counter and pulled out two plates after she locked the door. Slicing two large pieces of pie, she brought them to a table before running back behind the counter and appearing again with coloring books and pencils.

I sat in the booth opposite Tabby and picked up the fork, digging it into the pie. I hummed as the taste of apple spread across my tongue, making my taste buds tingle with delight.

"This is so good. Do you make it?" I asked.

Tabby grinned and nodded her head. "Yep. I make everything in the shop."

"You're very clever."

Her smile was huge when she looked over at me. "Why did you come to Lalbert?"

I sighed and put my elbow on the table as I rested my head on my hand. "My parents found my little stash and kicked me out," I said as tears welled up in my eyes with the sting I felt in my chest.

"Oh, Austen," Tabby gushed as she moved from her side of the bench and came to sit beside me. She put her arm around my shoulder just as the door unlocked and opened. "I'm sorry you have gone through that. I know that many people don't understand what it is to be little. But there isn't anything wrong with you."

I sighed and looked up as a man approached the table. "Hello there, has Tabby made a new friend?" he asked gently.

Tabby giggled and nodded her head. "Hi, Daddy. This is Austen, he is a little too, but his parents didn't understand his little side and kicked him out of his house. So, now he is coming to Lalbert."

Tabby's Daddy frowned and sighed. "I'm sorry, Austen, that you went through that. My name is Michael. As you've probably worked out, I'm Tabby's Daddy."

I tried to smile, but my heart was so sad that I struggled to smile. "Daddy, will you make us a chocolate milkshake?"

Michael smiled and leaned down to press a kiss on Tabby's lips. "Of course, I will, pretty girl. Then we will sit and have a bit of a grown-up conversation about where Austen will go so that we can help him."

Tabby smiled and bounced her head up and down. "Daddy will make sure you have somewhere to live. He has lots of contacts that can help you."

I breathed in deeply and slowly let it out. "Thank you, Tabby," I said quietly.

As it turned out, Tabby wasn't lying. Michael had loads of contacts. One of them was Asher, the owner of Club KINK. That very night, I found myself moving into an apartment above the club and being introduced to several different people who worked and lived there. Not only was Asher going to give me a house, but I now had a job. I was working behind the bar with Gunner and Jordan. Gunner was into puppy play, and Jordan was a kitten. They were lovely people, and I knew instantly that I'd found my home. It didn't completely take the sting away that my parents had caused. But it sure made it easier to cope with.

Chapter Five

"It's my party, it's my party," Jade sang as she spun around in her orange dress, making it swish around her knees. Her hair was pulled into pigtails on either side of her head. Her eyes were painted in sparkling eye shadow, and she had pink lipstick. We'd done our nails last night, Jade chose pink, and I chose blue. It was my favorite color.

"I'm so excited," I cried, joining in her dance with her. I was wearing my favorite party dress. It was blue with white flowers dotted around the hem. It had a lot of taffeta beneath it, making it flare out and feel like a princess ballerina dress. Jade had pulled my hair up into a ballet dancer bun, and I was wearing my pink ballet dancer flats to go with it.

"What time did Michael say he was coming to pick us up?" Jade asked as she looked at the clock with concern.

"Seven," I responded. "Michael is never late, so he will be here soon."

Jade nodded her head. "Do you think I'll get presents?"

"I bet you do. I bet that Gretel will bring you some of those yummy cookies that she makes. And Tabby will give you balloons or a stuffie." I giggled and bounced my head up and down.

Jade's eyes widened, and she gasped. "Oh, those cookies make me drool," she groaned, rubbing her belly. "Gretel is such a good cook."

"That's because her name is Gretel. The witch didn't really eat her and her brother Hansel. She taught them to cook all the sweet things her house was made of."

Jade gasped. "Do you think so?"

I laughed and nodded my head. "I know so. I saw the witch once."

"You did not. Wait. We are witches," Jade said before throwing her head back and cackling hysterically.

The door to my house opened, and I saw Tabby come running inside. She was dressed in a yellow party dress, and her hair was pulled up into pigtails like Jade. I hummed and wished I had the same hair.

"Hey, what's the matter, little one?" Michael asked as he came in and stood beside me.

"Tabby and Jade have the same hair, and mine is different," I huffed, folding my arms across my chest.

Michael chuckled. "Would you like your hair the same?"

I looked up at Tabby's Daddy and nodded my head.

"Alright, go and get me two matching hair bands and then come back; we have time to do your hair quickly; Tabby was over-excited, so we are early."

I squealed and went running towards my little room. I kept my particular room secret for me and the littles who came to visit me. I found the pretty blue bow bands and came running back toward Michael, who was now sitting on the couch.

"Sit down on the cushion," he said, pointing to the cushion between his legs. I did as I was told and leaned back against Michael's legs. With nimble fingers, he unthreaded my bun and pulled my hair into two pigtails.

"Look, Ione, look what Tabby gave me," Jade said excitedly as she showed me a pretty orange-colored stuffy kitten.

"That's so cute," I gushed. "What are you going to name your kitten?"

"Snagglepuss."

I giggled. "I like that," I said as Michael tapped my shoulder.

"There you go, hair in pigtails just like Tabby and Jade; now the, you three, let's get in the car. We have a party to attend."

Jade cheered and stood, clapping her hands. "Can I leave Snagglepuss here to keep him safe?"

I nodded my head. "Yep. You could put him with Ralph," I said. Ralph was my favorite stuffy. He was the first one I'd ever been given by Jade when she discovered I was a little.

"Good idea," Jade said as she turned and dashed into my little room, where Ralph was sitting on my bed. "Okay, Snagglepuss is safe. Ralph is going to look after him."

"Okay, now that we are all set, let's get going," Michael directed, ushering us out the front door and into his car.

Tabby, Jade, and I piled into the back seat before securing our seatbelts. "I'm so excited to go to your party, Jade. Thank you for inviting me," Tabby said.

Jade smiled. "That's okay. You and Ione are my bestest friends. I couldn't have a party without you two."

I grinned and leaned my head on Jade's shoulder. It was true she was my bestest friend. I loved her like a sister. I couldn't imagine life without her.

Chapter Six

L ennon

Walking into the club, I glanced around the room. Gunner was behind the bar with his collar firmly in place. Over the last couple of weeks, I'd started getting to know some of the members of Club KINK. From what I understood, a few of the more regular members were busy with a war that was coming between supernaturals and a Nephilim, Ettore. I'd heard about the war, but it wasn't in my mind. It meant that many old regulars weren't at the club anymore.

Asher, however, said they'd recently received a lot of new members and employees. Gunner told me that they had a fresh bartender start. His name was Austen, and he was a little. I was excited to be able to meet him.

"Hey Lennon, ready for the party?" Gunner called as I reached the bar.

I grinned and nodded. "I am. I came in earlier and helped March set up."

Littles loved puppies, and puppies loved the attention. A lot of times, littles and pups went hand in hand. Gunner's smile showed off the boisterous puppy he was.

"I went and checked it out; he went all out. Michael brought the food by earlier and then left to pick up Tabby. Have you had a chance to meet him yet?"

I nodded. "I met him and Tabby last week at the café. I thought I should go and introduce myself."

"They are a fantastic couple; they've been here since the start."

"Michael said that. Anyway, I best get into the room before the littles turn up and start destroying March's hard work."

"Definitely, Jade shouldn't be too far away."

I smiled and nodded before waving and walking towards the private rooms and the littles room. I saw Vaughn standing at the end of the hall, which I'd worked out quickly was his place. He was mated to a masochist named Aina. The guy was huge and imposing, but when I spoke to him, it surprised me how quietly spoken and submissive he was. I'd tried everything the BDSM world offered; it wasn't until I'd been in the scene for about ten years that I realized I was a Daddy.

"Hey, Vaughn," I called and waved at the giant troll.

His face lit up when he saw me and started down the hall toward me. "I hear we are having a birthday party today."

I nodded my head. "Yes, Jade. Her little one is turning three," I replied with a chuckle.

Vaughn grinned. He'd told me that he was pretty new to the world of BDSM. But with the help of Freya, the receptionist, and Domme, he'd discovered his kinks.

"From the amount of sugar I saw Michael bringing into the room with Asher, there are going to be some very hyper littles in there."

I groaned, making Vaughn laugh. "I don't envy you, man."

I chuckled. "I love it."

Vaughn smiled again. "I can see that. It takes a special person to be a Daddy or a Mommy. It's not for me," he said before shaking his head. "Well, no, that's not right. I like caring for Aina; I love the aftercare side. I like her cuddling to me."

I smiled warmly. "I can actually see that."

Vaughn smiled again and nodded his head. "I don't know. The aftercare stuff makes me feel important. Nurturing her. But I don't think I want a little."

"You can be a Daddy and not be into littles," I explained.

"Yeah?"

I nodded my head. "Sure can. It is about caring and nurturing. While your other mates might like the sadist side of BDSM, you get off on caring for her afterward and ensuring all her needs are taken care of."

Vaughn nodded, and his eyes widened. "Yeah, that's it. Man, I'm learning so much about myself since working here," he laughed.

I chuckled. "Places like this are great for teaching you about your likes and wants."

"That's true."

I grinned and nodded my head. "Anyway, I better get in there; I've got a few games I have to set up and prepare for the night."

"Alright, man, I'll talk to you later," Vaughn replied. As he walked to the end of the hall, he seemed lighter, as if he'd been thinking about the dilemma of being a Daddy for a while.

I chuckled as I walked into the little room, only to come to a screeching halt. The man looked up at me with big wide eyes. Sitting in the center of the room on a large plush red rug was a little with blonde curls, big blue eyes and the most cherub face I'd ever seen. His scent wrapped around me and filled me with want.

"Daddy," he whispered. I blinked and shook my head to clear it. Frowning slightly, I walked to the center of the room where the little one sat.

"What is your name?" I asked quietly as I moved onto the floor in front of him. Instantly he crawled towards me and into my lap. He was all arms and legs, and when I pulled him close, I could feel his diaper.

"Austen," he murmured around the stuffed pacifier in his mouth.

"Austen, I'm Lennon. You're an alpha," I mused. This was my mate. There was no questioning that scent, but Austen was an alpha.

"Yep," he said. "I got other mates coming, I think."

I chuckled and looked down at the little one in my lap. Breathing in deeply, I pressed my face into his hair. I wasn't necessarily expecting to find my little one tonight, yet here he was, in my lap, rubbing his face against my chest. Holy shit. My mate. My own little.

Chapter Seven

Austen

I'd arrived at the little room early. I wanted to get in my little space before others came. I was nervous and scared that the other littles wouldn't like me. It was a stupid thought, really, I had no reason to be rejected by them, but with the rejection from my parents, I wasn't sure how I felt.

I was sitting in the center of the room on a huge plush rug. I was dressed in my footy pajamas and a diaper on. I'd crawled around the room and looked at all the toys. But came back to the rug. As soon as Lennon walked into the room, his scent reached me, and I knew he was my mate. It took everything not to break out of my little space and stand running to him.

When he came and sat down, it'd been easy to climb into his lap. He smelled so good. Like what I could imagine a soft cloud would smell like. Rain after a hot day, wetting the concrete and settling the dust. I wanted to roll my body all over him and feel him all over me, inside and out.

Lennon was still stroking my hair when people came into the room. I looked up lazily and realized that the man was dressed in a diaper, mittens, and booties. He had a bonnet on his head. The woman smiled at us and came to join us on the rug.

"Hi there, my name is Acat, and this is my baby boy, Essia," she introduced. Essia was laid in her lap. "My boy is a baby, so he doesn't talk; how old is your boy?"

"Well, to be honest, I don't know; I've just met him and realized we were mates," Lennon answered.

Acat's eyes widened, and she grinned. "How wonderful. Can you talk, little one?" she asked.

I nodded my head. "I am one," I murmured around my pacifier, holding my fingers up to make a two.

Acat chuckled and nodded her head. "That's wonderful. Do either of you have an issue if I feed my baby?"

"No, not at all," Lennon replied before looking down at me. "Austen, I have to just pop you on the floor for now because I have to get some games ready for the birthday party."

I whimpered but nodded my head and moved off Daddy's lap. Daddy, not Lennon. He was my Daddy. I crawled over to sit beside Acat. My eyes widened slightly as she lifted her top and moved Essia's head so that he could suckle at her breast. I felt my cock stir at the public display.

"Do you have a Mommy?" she asked. I shook my head. "Oh, that's a shame. Do you drink out of a bottle or borrow a Mommy to feed you?"

My mouth watered. I loved being breastfed. It was something that helped me decide what age I was. There was something about being held and suckling on a breast, knowing how good it felt for Mommy too. I licked over my bottom lip as I watched Essia intently. His eyes closed, and his hand rested on his Mommy's other breast. She stroked her hand up and down his body, moving over the bottom of his diaper and back again. My cock was hard, and I unconsciously rocked back and forth, enjoying the feeling of my diaper cushioning my cock.

Daddy's scent surrounded me as he drew close. "Do you like watching Essia have his dinner?" he asked.

I looked at Daddy and noticed his eyes had darkened, and he was watching me with lust. I bit my bottom lip and nodded, rocking back and forth a little faster.

"Slow down, boy; I don't want you to spoil yourself just yet."

I whimpered and sighed but stopped rocking. I hoped that it meant that Daddy would help take care of me. I looked up as another man walked into the room.

"Lennon, thank you, man, for stepping in," the man said.

Daddy stood straight and went over to the man, shaking his hand. "Nash, don't mention it. I'm happy to do it."

Nash and Daddy started to chat about the plans for the night as my attention went back to Essia and his Mommy, Acat. My cock was painful, and I wanted relief, but I wanted to be a good boy for Daddy and not spoil myself too early.

Essia let go of his Mommy's breast and looked up at her. "Feel better, baby boy?" she asked tenderly.

Essia moaned and nodded his head. Acat smiled at her baby tenderly as another delicious scent wrapped around me, making me groan. When I looked over my shoulder, I saw a woman come to a screaming halt in the doorway. She stared with wide eyes between Lennon and me. I looked up at Daddy with shock on my face. How was this possible? Two mates in one night.

"Mommy," I cried, breaking the room's silence as I started moving on my hands and knees towards the woman with the beautiful scent of cinnamon surrounding her.

"You are my mate," she whispered.

I nodded my head. "And Daddy's."

The woman looked over at Daddy with shock on her face that was mirrored by Lennon's.

Daddy walked towards us and stuck out his hand. "I'm Lennon, and this is Austen. This is an extraordinary night. I've only just met Austen and realized we were fated, and now I realize I'm fated to you too."

Mommy nodded her head. "I'm Tanya. I don't really know what to say."

"Mommy and Daddy," I cooed with a smile. This night couldn't get any better.

Chapter Eight

T anya

The last thing I expected when I decided to come to Club KINK tonight was that I would be walking into the little room where I would be faced with my two mates. My mates. I'd been anticipating a night of fun at Jade's birthday party and watching the littles play. But now I was standing beside Lennon and Austen.

"What supernatural are you?" I asked Lennon.

"A phoenix shifter," he replied. "And you?"

"A witch."

"I'm a warlock," Austen murmured from where he was curled beside me in the beanbag we'd sat in.

"That will explain why three alphas are all mated. We will have to have a grown-up conversation at some stage," I said.

Austen smiled and bounced his head up and down. "That can wait until after the party," Lennon instructed.

"I agree. I hear that you are in charge of party games. What do you have planned?"

"Well, I was thinking of a game of passing the parcel. And I have another game in mind that involves donuts," Lennon chuckled. "I thought maybe we could also do some plaster painting and maybe a game of hide and seek."

"That sounds like a lot of fun. Have you been in the scene very long?" I smiled.

Lennon nodded his head. "About fifteen years. I didn't know I was a Daddy Dom until about five years ago. Did you always know you were a Mommy?"

I chuckled and shook my head. "No. In fact, I couldn't have ever imagined myself in age-play. I'd heard all the stigma that went with it and thought it was definitely not for me. But then, one night, they were holding a littles night, and Asher asked me if I'd like to participate. I said yes, just for shits and giggles, only to discover that age play wasn't the creepy world I thought it was."

Lennon laughed and nodded his head. "Yep. I get that. I was a bit the same too. I also stumbled into it before I realized it was for me."

I smiled. "My sister isn't going to believe me when I tell her that I have two mates," I chuckled before sobering quickly at the thought of Neveah. "I guess that is part of the grown-up conversation we need to have later."

"Your sister lives with you?" Lennon asked, picking up on my hesitancy.

"Yes. She is quadriplegic from a car accident she was in when she was a kid. Our parents died in the accident, so I'm all she has left. I live on the Devil's Advocates MC compound with her now, so it's made it a little easier; I've got a lot of people looking after her. But she is still my most important person."

Lennon nodded his head. "I'm glad that she has you. I don't know much about the Devil's Advocates. I've heard of them but haven't been in Lalbert long."

"Where were you before, Lalbert?"

"In Sydney," Lennon responded as he threaded his fingers through Austen's hair. It was strange; I'd met this man not twenty minutes earlier, yet I couldn't stop touching Austen. It felt so natural to be beside them and to be with them.

"Why made you leave?" I asked.

"Actually, my work. I'm a paramedic and wanted somewhere that was a little bit more relaxed. What I didn't realize when I applied for the job was the expected war coming."

"I'm surprised I haven't seen you at the hospital. I'm a doctor."

Lennon's eyes widened, and his mouth dropped open. "Really? That is weird. I'm there almost every day."

I frowned and shook my head. Mother fate worked in some strange ways. If I'd seen Lennon before, I would have known he was my mate. It was odd that we only met for the first time here.

I looked down at Austen, whose eyes closed and a slight smile on his face, enjoying the light scratches Lennon was running through his hair. "If you keep that up, our boy will fall asleep."

Lennon chuckled and glanced down at Austen. "I discovered that our boy likes breastfeeding."

My eyes flared. This was something I loved. It was part of the reason I'd held off on age play for so long. I had a nursing kink and worried that it made me sick. However, I didn't want to nurse children. I wished to nurse adults instead.

Austen's eyes opened, and when he looked up at me, I could see how much the idea turned him on. I moaned lightly. "I'm definitely going to feed my boy," I purred.

Austen smiled around his pacifier and snuggled closer to my chest. I chuckled and stroked my fingers down over his face. I couldn't believe that this was my life. There was so much we would have to work out, but I planned to enjoy every moment.

Chapter Nine

I one
"Here she is," Gunner cheered as we walked into the club. Jade squealed and ran towards the puppy as he wrapped his arms awkwardly around her over the bar.

"We'll meet you in the little room," Michael said as he took Tabby's hand and led her toward the little room.

"Happy birthday," Gunner said, kissing Jade on the cheek before turning to the fridge at the back of the bar and pulling out a sippy cup. "It has soda in it."

Jade's grin was wide as she took the sippy cup from him and brought it to her lips. Her eyes closed as she drank from the orange cup, and she moaned.

"Fanta," she said happily. Everything about Jade was orange. Her whole house was decorated in various shades of orange. Her little one loved the color.

"I'm glad you like it, but you better get into the little room; I think everyone is waiting for the birthday girl to arrive," Gunner said.

Jade nodded and turned around excitedly, reaching for my hand and starting across the club's main floor towards the hall that held the private rooms. KINK was busy tonight. There seemed to be people everywhere, and the sound of sex floated into the hallway.

"Happy birthday, little one," Asher said as he came down the hallway toward us.

"Thank you, Mr. Asher," Jade replied with a grin.

"Did you get spoiled?" Asher asked; his mate March stood beside him, dressed in a tight pair of shorts.

"I sure did," Jade said excitedly. "Ione bought me the biggest, hugest lollipop in the world. And Michael and Tabby got me a big stuffy kitten. I called him Snagglepuss."

Asher chuckled. "I love it. I think you have more presents waiting for you in the little room."

Jade's eyes widened further, and she gasped. "They brought me presents?"

Asher nodded his head. "Yep, I saw a few stuffies being taken in there."

Jade clapped her hands and bounced on her toes. "Come on, Ione, let's go meet our friends."

Jade bustled her way into the little rooms, but I came to a screaming halt and gasped. She grasped my hand and pulled me toward the littles room, making me giggle. I turned my head and waved to Asher and March, watching us with warm smiles.

"What? What is it?" Jade whispered as she looked at me with alarm on her face.

"My mates," I replied quietly.

"Who?" Jade asked as she glanced around the room.

I shrugged my shoulders. "I don't know. But Jade, I can scent them. It's beautiful."

Jade continued to look around the room. Everyone was either cuddling with the littles or playing with them. Tanya was sitting in a giant bean bag with a man I didn't recognize. He was laid across her lap, and she was nursing him. Another man sat beside her and stroked his fingers through the man's hair.

I continued to look around. My mate couldn't be Tanya; we played together in the past. I would have known if she was mine. But my eyes returned to the three sitting on the bean bag.

Suddenly the boy suckling on Tanya's breast lifted his head. He looked at me with dark eyes. The closer he got, the more I could scent that this man was indeed my mate. He crawled from Tanya's lap and said something quietly that I couldn't quite make out before he crawled to me.

"Is it him?" Jade asked, making me realize that she was still beside me.

"Yeah, and I think the other man and Tanya," I replied.

"Tanya? But you've played with her."

"I know. I don't understand," I answered, feeling my little side slip from me. I turned to face Jade, feeling guilty for pulling her out of her little space. But Jade seeming to be able to read my mind, shook her head and pulled me into a hug.

"Congratulations. Go get your mates; I'm fine," she said, kissing me on the cheek.

I nodded my head and watched as Jade walked deeper into the room. Acat recognized her and called out. "Happy birthday, little one."

Jade's grin spread across her face as she bounded toward Acat, making me feel better about her being able to fall back into her little space so easily. I turned my attention back to the man that had crawled and now sat at my feet. I lowered to the ground beside him, and the man wrapped his arm around my shoulders and pulled me into a hug.

"My mate," he said.

I groaned. The scent of him was so strong, and I wanted him. Thankfully I took heat suppressants so I wouldn't go into heat. But I still wanted desperately to be close to this man.

"What's your name?" I asked.

"Austen, what's yours?"

"Ione."

"You a little?"

I nodded my head and bit my lip. "Is Tanya and that man your Mommy and Daddy?"

Austen nodded his head. "Our Mommy and Daddy."

I frowned and shook my head. "I've played with Tanya; she isn't fated with me."

Austen smiled and shook his head. "That's because you both needed all of us to be together."

My eyes widened. "I thought it was only dragons that were affected like that."

Austen shook his head again. "No. It can happen to any supernatural. It's just how Mother fate works."

I smiled and nodded my head. "Come and meet Lennon, our Daddy."

I nodded and stood before following Austen over to where Tanya sat with Lennon. Mommy and Daddy. It was strange. I'd longed for this kind of relationship for as long as I'd known I was a little, but now it was here; I was scared.

"Hi, little one," Tanya said with a smile. This close, her scent of cinnamon and apples wrapped delicately around me.

"Hi, you're my Mommy. You've always been my Mommy."

Tanya chuckled. "So, it seems. We will have a grown-up talk later. But this is Lennon; he is mine and Austen's mate."

I turned to Daddy and inhaled. "You're my Daddy."

Daddy looked at me and smiled, nodding his head. "That's right. We will definitely talk later, but I have some games to start now that the birthday girl is here."

I grinned and took Daddy's seat as he climbed out of the bean bag and walked over to Jade, handing her a large orange stuffed lion. Jade squealed and hugged Daddy around the middle. I was surprised I wasn't jealous of the action, but I trusted Jade implicitly. I knew she wouldn't try to take my Daddy.

Mommy stroked her fingers through my pigtails. "Your hair looks so pretty like this."

I turned and grinned at Mommy. "Thank you. Michael did it for me to match Jade and Tabby."

Austen climbed into my and Mommy's lap before lifting Mommy's top so he could suckle on her breast. I felt my pussy give a hard throb at sight. Automatically I reached out and ran my hands up and down Austen's legs. He moaned and moved his hips back and forth. I moved my hand down over his front and felt that he wore a diaper beneath his overalls.

Austen moaned. "That feels good," he said as I pushed on the front of his diaper.

Mommy looked at us and smiled. "I like watching you two play."

"Will you want to play further?" I asked Austen.

He nodded his head and bit into his bottom lip. "Yes," he said with a husky voice.

I smiled. I couldn't wait to show them my little room. It wasn't just a room filled with toys. There were toys in there, but there was also an extensive array of spicy toys. They were my favorite.

Chapter Ten

Austen

The rest of the night was a lot of fun. I laid with Mommy while Daddy ran games for the littles. I couldn't quite comprehend this was my life. I had met not just one fated mate but three. My dick throbbed by the night's end, and I was desperate for something. I knew the minute I was touched, I would explode.

"I think we need to find somewhere that we can get relief, but then talk," Mommy said to Daddy.

"I agree; I'll see if one of the private rooms is empty." Daddy left the littles room and was back after a few moments. "Found one."

Ione hugged her friend, Jade, goodbye and came over to us. "We need some private family time," Daddy told Ione.

She smiled and nodded her head. My body felt like it was hard-wired. I didn't know what would happen, but I needed relief. I needed something. Daddy took Ione's hand while Mommy took mine. They led us from the room, and we went to a private room. Once inside, Daddy shut and locked the door. The room was filled with a large bed in the center, with couches on either side.

"I don't want to pull you both out of your little spaces, but I think we need to talk first," Lennon said.

I stood and nodded my head. "I think that's a good idea," I replied as the little space slipped.

Lennon nodded his head and went to sit on the couch. Tanya sat beside him while Ione and I took the couch opposite.

"The main thing I need to know is what you want," Lennon said.

Ione frowned and shook her head. "Do you mean as in us?" she asked.

Lennon nodded his head. "This is a big thing. We aren't just talking about mating; we are talking about taking our lifestyle in a new direction. I need to know if you do this regularly or if you only want to play at certain times."

"Firstly, I want to mate with all of you," Ione started. "Secondly, my little side is fairly ingrained in my everyday life. It's not something I take to work with me, but I have a little room in my home, and I like to be little when I'm home."

Lennon nodded his head. "What about you, Austen?"

I breathed in deeply before slowly letting it out. "I came to Lalbert because my parents discovered my box of little things and kicked me out. They thought I was a pedophile. Before then, I had only played occasionally when I had the house. But it is something I would like to do more regularly. Coming to Lalbert has helped with that."

"I'm sorry you went through that," Tanya sighed. "Unfortunately, this is the problem with age play. A lot of people don't understand it."

I nodded my head. The sting of my parent's rejection was slowly healing, but it still hurt to think about that day. I'd not heard from them at all. I kept hoping that I might get a phone call or something, but nothing was coming.

"I am a Daddy full time in my off time. I love caring for a little one. I just haven't had one of my own," Lennon said.

"I'm the same," Tanya said. "I did have a little, but he cheated on me. My biggest issue is that I work long hours, so I don't have much time at home."

"Maybe that is why Mother fate chose all four of us to be mated?" Ione said. "Where you don't have the constant time, we have two a Mommy and Daddy."

Tanya smiled and nodded her head. "That's quite possible."

"The other thing we need to discuss is what is off limits," Lennon said.

"I am sexual in both little and adult space," Ione said. "I have a lot of toys at home that is sex toys as well."

Lennon nodded his head and glanced over at me. "Wearing a diaper makes me hard. I don't have a lot of experience. I'm fairly new to everything. But I like to play even when I'm in little space."

Lennon nodded as well. Tanya smiled over at him. "I like to nurse. It is one of my main kinks. I've nursed Ione before, and tonight I nursed you, Austen."

"I'm not so much in the nursing. I don't mind it now and then, but it's not a big kink for me," Ione said.

"It is for me," I said with a chuckle, making Tanya laugh.

"I worked that one out," she laughed.

I grinned. "Can we mate now?" I asked.

Lennon groaned and nodded his head.

"I think we should show the kids how Mommy and Daddy do it," Tanya said as she stood from the couch and lifted her skirt to reveal she didn't have panties on beneath and straddled Lennon's knee. He moaned and stroked his hands up her thighs; holding her hips, he ground her hard down his lap.

I licked over my bottom lip. Fuck, that was sexy to watch.

Chapter Eleven

Tanya

I straddled Lennon's lap and heard Austen's groan as Lennon ran his hands up my thighs and exposed my ass.

"Fuck, you're sexy," Lennon growled as I reached down and stripped out of my shirt. I smiled and continued to roll my hips against his crotch. His hard cock pressed against my bare pussy, making me wetter. The scent of my arousal floated through the air.

There was much more to talk about, but I couldn't hold back any longer. I needed to make these three my mates. Lennon stroked his hands up over my ass and spread my cheeks. I knew that Austen and Ione were getting a view of me opened wide to them.

"What do you want to do, Austen?" Ione asked.

"I want to lick Mommy's ass," he answered.

Ione moaned. "Can I rub you through your diaper?"

"Yes, please," he answered. I looked over my shoulder as Austen climbed from the couch and crawled over to where Lennon and I were sitting.

"Wait a minute, let me take my skirt off, and Daddy can get undressed," I directed.

Austen waited patiently as I slipped my skirt from my body, and Lennon quickly stripped out of his clothes before sitting naked.

"Daddy's cock is big," Austen whispered loudly to Ione.

When I looked over at Ione, she nodded her head. "I like it," she whispered back.

"Me too," Austen replied. I straddled Lennon's lap again and turned my head to watch Austen pull his clothes off until he was just dressed in his diaper. He'd lost his pacifier and crawled toward us.

I leaned forward against Lennon's chest. "Eat, Mommy," I directed to Austen, who moaned. He didn't have to be asked twice. My eyes rolled as I felt his tongue penetrate my pussy before licking up over my back entrance.

Lennon grunted as Austen's tongue slipped over his shaft and balls before working back to my ass. Austen moaned, and when I looked over my shoulder, I could see that Ione had worked for her hand down beneath his diaper and was stroking him.

"I want to watch," I said as I stood from Lennon's lap and turned; I sat back down and slipped Lennon's cock between my thighs.

Austen moaned and licked up Lennon's shaft before circling his tongue around my clit.

"Fuck, that feels good, baby; you lick me so good," Lennon grunted as Austen's tongue roved up and down his shaft.

I'd played with littles for years, but something in this moment was so much sexier. I'd never been so turned on in my life. My pussy was dripping. The curls that sat nestled between my legs were soaked.

Austen's eyes were glazed as he rocked back and forth into Ione's hand.

"Austen, sweetie, I think you need to help sissy out of her pretty dress," I directed.

Austen turned and nodded his head. Ione turned to him and allowed him to unzip her dress before she pushed it down over her body and off onto the floor. Her pretty lace panties were soaked.

"You smell so good," Austen moaned.

"You should taste her. Tell Daddy what she tastes like," Lennon growled.

Austen licked over his bottom lip before pulling at Ione's panties and slipping them onto the floor. I reached between my legs and stroked up and down Lennon's cock. She widened and her legs and the scent of her arousal filled the air around us. My mouth watered at the thought of having her bald pussy smothering my face.

Slapping the head of his cock against my clit I rocked back and forth. Austen bent forward and licked up and down Ione's cunt as she widened her legs and tilted her head on her shoulders. A long moan fell from her lips as Austen lapped at her like a starving man.

I couldn't take it anymore; lifting my hips, I tilted the head of Lennon's cock and slid down on him. The stretch of him as he entered me was everything. I moaned as I rocked back and forth, feeling him fill me completely.

"Fuck I want to see you with Austen's cock deep in your asshole with me in your cunt," Lennon growled into my ear.

"Yes," I hissed at the image that floated into my mind.

Austen laid flat on the floor and continued to lap at Ione's pussy as he thrust into the floor.

"I think our boy needs to cum," I said.

Ione moved from her spot in front of Austen and pushed on his back to keep him flat. Straddling his hips, she thrust down into his diaper-clad ass. Rubbing her clit against his ass. Austen let out a long moan, and I felt our magic start to move around the room. I watched as the auras of Austen and Ione moved and began to dance together. Ione's face was lifted to the sky as she moved hard against Austen's ass. With a sudden strength, Austen spun beneath Ione, lifting her quickly and placing her beneath him. With nimble fingers, he tore a hole in his diaper and pulled his cock through the hole. Lifting Ione's legs in the sky, he plunged deep inside her.

Ione cried out and clawed at Austen's back. Their auras danced higher and higher into the sky. Without further warning, Ione thrust her hand against Austen's chest and screamed as her orgasm and power washed over them. Austen returned the mating mark by pressing on Ione's chest. He growled as he came over and over, filling Ione with his cum.

I felt Lennon's teeth penetrate me just as Austen pulled out of Ione and stripped from his diaper. Turning enough to press my hand to Lennon's chest, I called forward my return mating mark as my orgasm flooded my body. My juices poured down over Lennon's shaft, coating his thighs. Lennon's roars shook the room. As soon as our mating marks locked in place, I climbed from Lennon and pulled Austen to me. Lennon moved from the couch and lifted Ione to the bed. He wrapped her legs around his neck as he fucked hard into her. Ione was screaming in pleasure.

"Come here, baby, fuck your Mommy," I demanded.

Austen didn't need to be told twice. He filled me at once and fucked me hard.

"Harder, Austen, I want you to fuck me with everything you have," I growled. Austen snapped his hips hard against me. "Yes, fuck me, just like that."

My boy didn't disappoint as he fucked me hard. I wrapped my fingers into his hair, tugging on the long strands. Our magic combined as my orgasm peaked. I pressed my hand against his chest and pushed my magic into him. Austen roared as he answered the mark. Slowly he rolled off me, and I walked on unsteady legs toward the bed. Lennon was fucking into Ione like a man had. Her nails gouged into his back, and her toes were curled.

"Mommy, I need you," she cried. I slid my hand between the two and pressed my fingers against Ione's clit. "Yes, yes, yes."

I watched as Austen's teeth extended and knew he was about to mark Ione. Slipping my hand from her pussy, I brought it up to her chest and allowed my magic to work. Ione screamed so loudly it echoed through the room as her orgasm washed over her.

Austen had moved over to the bed and climbed on his hands and knees. As soon as Lennon moved from Ione, Austen dipped his fingers into her pussy and took the juices of her and Lennon before spreading them across his asshole. Lennon groaned and flipped Austen to his back.

"I want to see your face when I fuck you," he growled.

Austen's eyes rolled in his head as Lennon gently entered him. Slowly and languidly, he fucked our boy. Austen's magic was strong, and I could see he was close. Almost reverently, Lennon leaned forward and bit into

Austen's chest. Austen cried out as he thrust his hand against Lennon's chest.

Slowly we all came back to earth. "My god, we are mated," Ione said with a giggle.

"Any regrets?" I asked, looking down at her.

She shook her head. "Not a single regret. But now we have to talk logistics."

I sighed and nodded. "I guess we do. I also need to tell you three that I have an added complication. I have a sister who is disabled. She is quadriplegic and relies on me for her care. She currently lives with me at the Devil's Advocates compound."

"That doesn't bother me," Austen said. "Does she know about your lifestyle?"

I shook my head. "No. She knows I come to the club, but I've never told her about being a Mommy."

"Do you think she would understand?" Ione asked.

I sighed and shrugged my shoulders. "I don't know to be honest. I guess I'm going to have to have a conversation with her. But the biggest problem we have is where we are going to live. I'm happy to stay on the compound, but wherever we live, I have to take Neveah into account."

"Of course, we wouldn't expect any less," Lennon said.

"The only thing I need to warn you about the Devil's Advocates compound is that they are preparing for the war between supernaturals and the Nephilim Ettore. Currently, at the compounds, the gods are living there too."

Lennon's eyes widened, and his mouth dropped open. "Wait, the gods? As in the god gods."

I chuckled and nodded my head. "Yes, the gods, god, as in Odin, Hel, Hades, and the rest. Including Lucifer."

"Holy shit," Lennon whispered. "That makes me want to live there even more."

"Me too," Austen replied.

"I'm happy to live there, but I don't want to be involved in the war," Ione answered.

"You don't have to be. Nobody is enforcing it. In fact, the gods have even sent people to Middle Earth who doesn't want to be involved."

"Wait, we could go to Middle Earth?" Austen gushed.

I nodded my head. "Yes. If we asked Odin, we could."

Austen looked at Ione and Lennon. "Do you want to go to Middle Earth?"

Ione frowned. "But what about work and Jade?"

Austen hummed. "Well, Jade could come."

"As for work, you don't have to worry about that, the gods have everything prepared on Middle earth, but if you wanted to stay here, you are welcome to; we won't go unless everyone wants to go."

"Can I think about it?" Ione asked.

"Of course, you can. This isn't something that should be made quickly," Lennon said, glancing over at me. I nodded my head. He was right; such a big decision couldn't be made on a whim. Not to mention I had to find out if Neveah would even want to leave earth side to go to Middle Earth.

Chapter Twelve

I one
My mind was going over and over what Tanya had suggested. Could I pack up and leave earth to move to another world. I wasn't sure. The one thing that kept bringing me back was Jade. Could I leave Jade behind? I wasn't sure I could. I knew how hurt she would be if I went, but was it right to live my life for Jade, now that I was mated?

When I arrived at work on Monday, Jade was sitting at my desk with a broad smile on her lips.

"Alright, girl, spill the details," she said with a grin, causing me to giggle.

"I had a perfect weekend. I've got three mates," I said with a sigh. After leaving the club, we all returned to Tanya's home. Her sister was spending the night with her friend Autumn. We were introduced to her on Sunday. Neveah was an adorable girl. She was older than I'd anticipated. When Tanya told me she had a sister, I was expecting a toddler. But Neveah was seventeen years old. She wasn't able to care for herself at all. When Tanya wasn't home caring for her, Neveah had help from other members of the Devil's Advocates. But with the coming war, Tanya told us she was worried about what would happen to Neveah.

I worried about it too. I knew that if we went to Middle Earth, Neveah would be safe, but the other issue was that Tanya was a doctor, and Lennon was a paramedic. There was a good chance they would be needed for the war. I wasn't sure what the right thing to do was.

"You look like you are thinking about something tough," Jade said.

I sighed and nodded my head. "I am. Tanya said something on the weekend that has me thinking, and I'm unsure what the right answer is."

"Want to share it?"

"You've heard about the war expected to be between the supernaturals and the Nephilim Ettore?"

Jade nodded her head. We hadn't heard much about it, but it was something we'd known about for a while. Well, not necessarily the war, but the Nephilim Ettore. We learned about him and Morpheus because they often got supernatural children from the orphanages and made them fight or bred them. Luckily for me, I was a run-of-the-mill witch, so it was never very important to Ettore.

"Well, I spent the weekend at the Devil's Advocates compound, where Tanya lives, and the gods are all there."

Jade's eyes widened, and her mouth dropped open. "Are you shitting me?"

I shook my head. "Nope. I met Hel, Hades, and Frigg while there, and I literally had dinner with Odin sitting at the same table as me."

"Fucking hell, which is awesome," Jade exclaimed.

"It was kind of cool. But anyway, Tanya was telling us that Odin had made an offer to those possibly involved in the war, particularly those on the Devil's Advocates compound and Onyx Rebels, that if we didn't want to fight, he would allow us to go to Middle Earth to live."

Jade's face was covered with shock. "Are you going to go?"

I shrugged my shoulders. "That's my dilemma. I don't know. There is so much to think about. Austen and Lennon have both said they would happily go. But Tanya is a doctor; I think she would be needed here when the war comes. And Lennon is a paramedic; he will be needed too. Then there is Tanya's sister, Neveah. She is quadriplegic and needs care, it would be better for her to be on Middle Earth, but I'm worried about her being on her own if we don't all go. The final thing I'm worried about is you. I don't want to be separated, but I don't know if I could be selfish enough to ask you to come."

"Okay," Jade interrupted, holding her finger up. "First, don't you dare waste time worrying about me. I will follow you wherever, even to Middle Earth. I trust you, and I trust the gods. I know that we would be protected."

I nodded my head. It was true; from what the gods said, I knew we would be safe on Middle Earth. There was no way that Ettore could get there.

"As for Tanya and Lennon, you can't control what they want to do. If they choose to go to Middle Earth, that is their decision. But you are right, Neveah needs help, and it would be unfair to send her to Middle Earth alone. She will need someone with her."

I sighed. "I just don't know. I mean, it's scary. It's scary to think about going to a whole other world, but at the same time, I'm terrified to stay. I don't want to be involved in a war. One day I want to be able to have children, and the thought of my mates being potentially killed or injured in a war is horrifying."

Jade nodded her head. "I understand. What is your gut telling you."

"Honestly? It's telling me to go."

"Then do it. Take the chance. It's not forever. You will be able to come back here one day. It won't hurt to go there. Consider it an experience to tell your grandchildren."

I chuckled and nodded my head. "And you would come with us?"

"Try and hold me back," she said with a wink.

Lennon

It was hard to believe that I was now a mated man to not just one but three other people. I couldn't believe my luck. I was in awe about the whole lot. My life was so different from what I'd imagined. We'd had been mated for just over a year. Not only was I mated, man, but I had also been living in Middle Earth for a year. The thought of returning earthside wasn't a prospect I really wanted to think about. From what I'd heard, the war was raging, and what we would return to wasn't going to be the same as what we'd left. But I was safe. My mates were safe, and Neveah was safe.

At first, it took a lot to get used to living on Middle Earth. There was enough for everyone. Most of the people that were here were omegas. We all worked jobs to help one another. There was complete equality, and it was the epitome of paradise. Tanya had taken longer to get used to it than I did. She was so used to being on the go and working hard that Middle Earth felt like a holiday.

We found our groove after about a month of being on Middle Earth. Tanya and I started teaching basic first aid and health to those who wanted to learn, while Austen worked in the gardens, growing all the food we could ask for. Ione helped to teach the children along with Jade. They were excellent teachers, and the kids adored them. We found our place, and I couldn't be happier.

Even Neveah seemed more at ease than I'd ever seen before. Autumn came with us to Middle Earth, which didn't surprise me. I got the distinct feeling that the two of them were fated and would be mated one day. Autumn did everything for Neveah and took care of her so much that Tanya was freed. At first, it had felt strange to Tanya not to have to care for Neveah. She found herself getting irritated with Autumn, but after sitting and talking it out with Neveah she realized that Neveah was growing up. It was time for Tanya to pull back a bit.

The day we found that the two of them were pregnant our celebrations could probably be heard earthside. It was perhaps easier when she discovered that she and Ione were expecting a baby each. They were both so excited. I wasn't sure if Tanya or Ione had wanted children, but the minute we found out they were pregnant, my questions were answered with their excitement.

"Ready to push, little one?" I asked as I stroked a hand over Ione's face, which was coated in sweat.

"I'm ready," she said quietly, gritting her teeth as she bore down. Diana, the goddess of birth, was sitting between Ione's legs, ready to catch our baby as they came into the world.

"That's it, Ione; give me one big huge push, and the baby will be here," she encouraged.

Ione clasped my hand tight, squeezed her eyes closed, and pushed. I watched in awe as the baby slipped from my mate into Diana's waiting arms.

"You have a little boy," Diana exclaimed happily. "And he is a warlock."

Gently she placed our son on Ione's chest. Ione looked down into our son's face and kissed the top of his head. Tanya and Austen stood on the other side of the bed. Tanya held our daughter, a phoenix shifter we'd named Lucy, in her arms. Lucy was born three days earlier.

"What are we going to name him, little one?" Tanya asked as she pressed a kiss to Ione's temple.

"Oscar," Ione answered.

"Oscar, it is," I answered. "What do you think, Austen? You like Oscar for your son's name?"

Austen looked up at me with wide eyes. "He's my baby," he gushed.

I chuckled and nodded my head. "We have two very healthy babies."

Three mates and two children. I couldn't ask for a better life.

The end.

Don't miss out!

Visit the website below and you can sign up to receive emails whenever S L Davies publishes a new book. There's no charge and no obligation.

https://books2read.com/r/B-A-NZRR-CSUDC

BOOKS2READ

Connecting independent readers to independent writers.

Did you love *Ione*? Then you should read *Maid for the Doms*[1] by S L Davies!

Alaina had been desperate for a job, but when the job as a maid for two wealthy and reclusive brothers came up, she jumped at the chance. Not only did it give her a job, It also gave her a place to stay. What Alaina never anticipated was the extra activities that these brothers enjoyed. A lifestyle that was not only intriguing but one she would come to desire.

This was previously released as an anthology story in 2019. There are possibly triggering subjects. Language and themes suited to 18+

Read more at https://www.amazon.com/~/e/B0832T8F7Z.

---

1. https://books2read.com/u/mqXWeZ

2. https://books2read.com/u/mqXWeZ

Also by S L Davies

Breeding Facility
Memphis
Bacchus
Coltrane
Pax
Raiden
Nash
Breeding Facility

Cold Case
Cold Case
Cold Mystery

Devil's Advocates
Lynx
Israel
Jai
Jasper
Arley
Zion

Kaki

Scout

Rigby Brothers

Asher

Burgess

Macklin

Drake

Jericho

Obsidian

River of Lies

River of Lies

Schiavu

Schiavu

Shifter Ink

Brenton

Chase

Orion

Sloane

Sahara

Stolen

Stolen
The Murphy Princess
Little Warrior

Wild Claw Pack
Connell
Ward
Fenris
Herrick

Standalone
Sisters Revenge
Killer Love
Soldiers At War
Second Chances
Bunny
Caged
By The Sword
The Cult
Rising Sun
Forbidden Bound
Christmas Escape
Executioner
Maid for the Doms
Call of the Gods
Coroner
Moon Waker

Watch for more at https://www.amazon.com/~/e/B0832T8F7Z.

About the Author

S L Davies is an Australian Author living in Country, Victoria. She is inspired by the world around her.

Read more at https://www.amazon.com/~/e/B0832T8F7Z.